Y0-BED-181

TU TZE-CHUN

杜子美

TU TZE-CHUN

by RYŪNOSUKE AKUTAGAWA

translated by DOROTHY BRITTON

with woodcuts by NAOKO MATSUBARA

and an introduction by E.G. SEIDENSTICKER

KODANSHA INTERNATIONAL LTD: PUBLISHERS
Tokyo, Japan

JAPAN PUBLICATIONS TRADING COMPANY: DISTRIBUTORS
Rutland, Vermont, U.S.A.

Published by Kodansha International Ltd.
with editorial offices at 3-19 Otowa-machi,
Bunkyo-ku, Tokyo, Japan

Kodansha International Ltd. books are distributed outside of Japan by: Japan Publications Trading Company, P.O. Box 469, Rutland, Vermont, U.S.A. or C.P.O. Box 722, Tokyo, Japan.

Library of Congress Catalog Card No. 65- 12283

First edition, 1965

Printed in Japan.

INTRODUCTION

AMONG modern Japanese writers whose reputations can be thought established beyond shaking, Akutagawa Ryūnosuke stands out as something of a sport. He differs from his fellows, in the first place, in his concentration upon the short story, and it is safe to say that he is the most important modern Japanese writer who produced no long fiction. He stands out, secondly, in that most of his writing is very far removed indeed from the autobiographical fiction that has so dominated modern Japanese literature. And, finally, he was the first writer to take advantage of the riches to be found in the Oriental classics.

He was a virtuoso writer, changing his style and point of view to suit the situation—Chinese, ancient Japanese, Indian, or, perhaps most remote and esoteric of all, Christian. Yet he never seemed quite sure of himself and his writing. His mother was insane, and all his life he was haunted by a fear that the ailment might be hereditary; and he always seemed to feel a little guilty about his writing. It was as if, in choosing his distant, classical themes, he were abdicating the recognized duty of a writer, the duty to report on the facts of his own experience. He is on record as thinking Shiga Naoya, a contemporary who specialized in autobiographical fiction, to be a superior writer to himself, and toward the end of his life he also took to writing autobiographical sketches. Although they do not succeed as fiction, some of them are fascinating and horrifying documents, for the reader has before him the spectacle of a brilliant mind going to pieces. Finally in 1927, at the age of thirty-four, Akutagawa killed himself.

In some of his classical adaptations he left the story fairly well alone, but treated the characters as if they were modern, able to view one another and themselves in the light of modern psychology. In others he changed the story. "Tu Tze-chun," which was written in 1920, falls into the second category. It has a ninth-century Chinese model, but the Chinese version is longer and more complicated, and lacks the bland, mildly happy ending. Akutagawa cut it in half and sealed the wound in his own fashion, and so produced an altogether more human story than his Chinese predecessor.

The story is illustrated with the very unusual and exquisitely conceived woodblock prints of Matsubara Naoko, about whom the master of woodblock prints in Japan, Munakata Shikō, has written: "It is very rare in Japan to find a woman woodblock print artist who produces with such powerful and voluminous creativity. It can even be said that she is the first woman artist to display such qualities. Artists who are able to create balance between black and white, boldly and without fear, and so enhance the pure qualities of the print, are extremely rare...."

Of Miss Britton's translation nothing need be said save that it is a rare piece of good luck to have a translation by a gifted writer who is also a native speaker of the original language. I have no doubt that other readers will be as impressed with it as I was.

E.G. SEIDENSTICKER

Tokyo, 1964

[NOTE: *Japanese names mentioned in the introduction appear as they would in Japanese, with family name first.*—Editor]

ONE spring day, at sunset, a young man stood under the West Gate of the T'ang city of Loyang, vacantly looking up at the sky. The young man's name was Tu Tze-chun, and although he was the son of a rich man, he had spent all of his inheritance, and now, being without even the price of a night's lodging, he was in a piteous state.

Loyang in those days was a city at the very height of its prosperity, whose equal could not be found anywhere, and its streets were full of people and carriages incessantly passing to and fro. In the oily light of the setting sun, which bathed the whole gate, the gauze hats of the old men, the golden earrings of the Turkish women, and the colored bridles adorning the white horses made a beautiful picture as they flowed along without ceasing. But in spite of all this, Tu Tze-chun just leaned against the wall of the gate and gazed vacantly at the sky. In the sky, through the streaming mist, a thin moon floated, faintly white, like the imprint of a fingernail.

"The day wanes. I am hungry. Yet there is no one who would be likely to take me in.... Rather than live and know such misery, would it not be far better to throw myself into the river and die?" Wild thoughts like these had been going through his head for some time.

Suddenly, there stood before him an old man with a squint. In the light of the setting sun, he cast an enormous shadow on the gate. He had paused and was looking intently at Tu Tze-chun.

"What are you thinking?" he demanded.

"Were you speaking to me? I have nowhere to sleep tonight, and I was wondering what to do." The old man's question had been so abrupt that Tu Tze-chun simply lowered his eyes and, without thinking, told him the truth.

"So that's it. Poor fellow!"

The old man thought for a while, and presently pointed to the sunlight shining on the road.

"I'll tell you a secret. Stand in the light of the setting sun and let your shadow fall on the ground. Dig at midnight at the spot where the shadow of your head came, and you are bound to find a cartload of gold."

"I shall?"

Tu Tze-chun raised his eyes in amazement. But the strange thing was that the old man was nowhere to be seen, nor anyone resembling him in the slightest. In the sky the moon looked even whiter than before, and in addition to the never-ending movement of people in the street, two or three excitable bats were already circling about.

In the space of one day, Tu Tze-chun became the richest man in Loyang. Following the old man's instructions, he let the setting sun cast his shadow on the ground, and at midnight when he secretly dug at the spot where the shadow of his head had fallen, he found a pile of gold so large that a mammoth cart would not hold it all.

The now wealthy Tu Tze-chun immediately bought himself a fine mansion, and began to lead a life of luxury not even outdone by that of the Emperor Hsuan Tsung himself. He imported fine wines from Lanling, and *lung-yen* fruit from far Kweichow, and in his gardens he planted peonies that changed color four times a day, while countless white peacocks roamed freely in and out among them. He collected gems, and commissioned brocades and embroideries; he had carriages made of aromatic woods, and chairs of ivory. If I enumerated all of his extravagances, this tale would never be finished.

Word got around, and acquaintances who previously would not even have greeted him in the street came flocking day and night to pay their respects. The number increased daily, and before six months had passed, there was not one among the many celebrated wits and beauties of Loyang who had not been to Tu Tze-chun's house.

And for these guests, Tu Tze-chun daily gave wine feasts. It is impossible to describe the abundance of these affairs. In brief, let me say only that Tu Tze-chun used to serve European wines in golden goblets, and while magicians from India entranced the guests with their sword swallowing, twenty maidens, ten with jade lotus flowers in their hair and ten with agate peonies, played delightful melodies on the flute and zither.

But no matter how rich one can be, sooner or later money comes to an end, and so naturally, even the magnificent House of Tu Tze-chun in a year or two became quite poor, and when that happened, since mankind is fickle, even friends who had come daily until yesterday passed his door without so much as a greeting. And so it was that in the spring of the third year, Tu Tze-chun once again was completely bankrupt, and in the whole wide city of Loyang, there was not one house that would even give him a cupful of water, let alone shelter for the night.

As evening drew on, he made his way once more to the West Gate of Loyang, and stood there gazing vacantly at the sky, not knowing which way to turn. And once again, just as before, there was the old man with the squint, and what did he do but ask, "What are you thinking?"

Tu Tze-chun glanced at the old man's face, then averted his eyes, abashed, and did not reply. But the old man repeated his question with such kindness that Tu Tze-chun gave the same reply as before.

"I have nowhere to sleep tonight and was wondering what to do."

"So that's it. Poor fellow! I'll tell you a secret. Stand in this light from the setting sun, and when your shadow strikes the ground, dig at midnight where your heart was. There's sure to be a cartload of gold buried there."

The old man had no sooner spoken than he disappeared into the throng of people as if he had been erased.

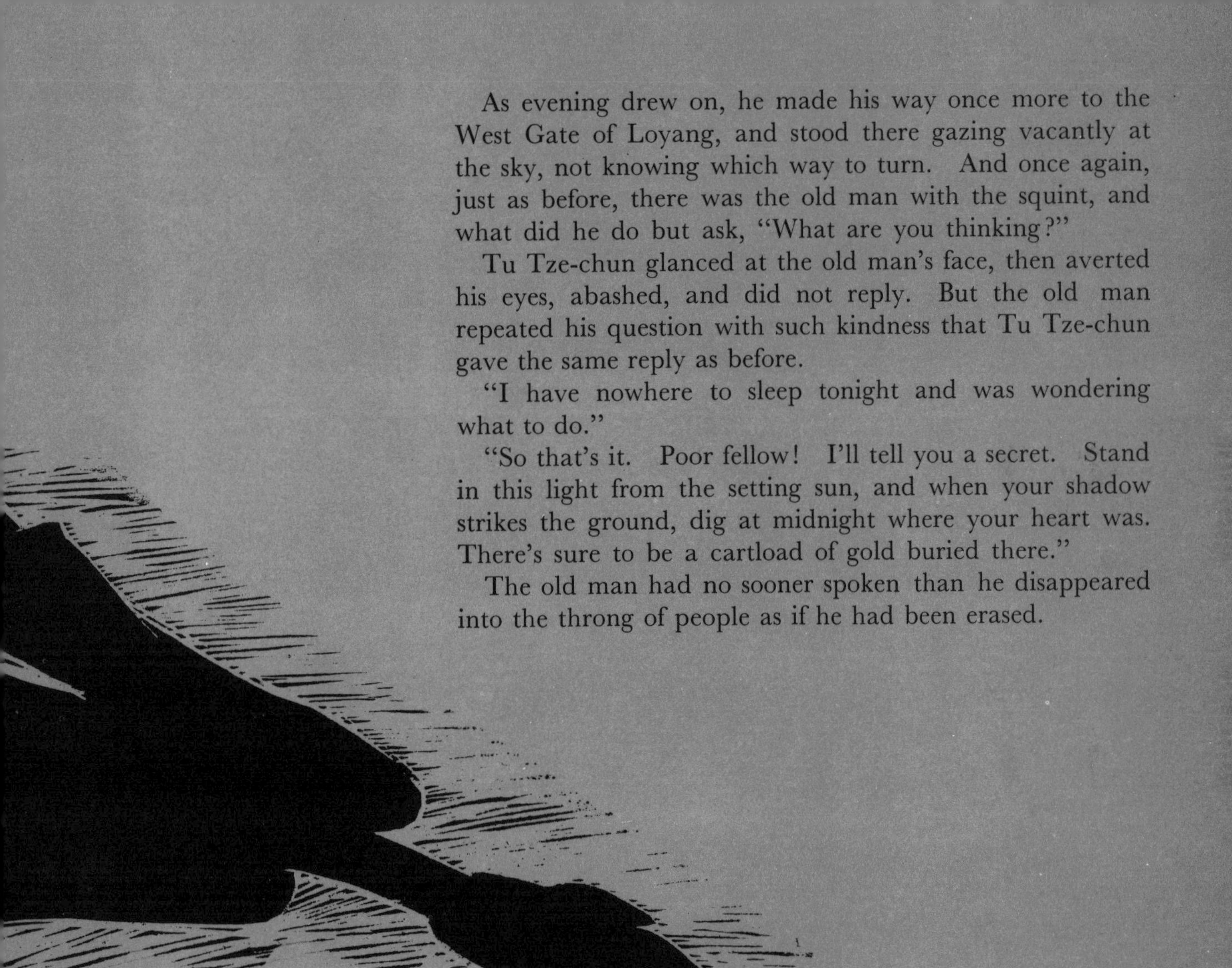

The very next day, Tu Tze-chun was once more the richest man in China, and immediately began to live extravagently. The peonies in his garden, and among them white peacocks sleeping, the magicians from India who could swallow swords—all was the same as before. And in three years, the immense cartload of gold was completely gone.

"What are you thinking?"

The old man with a squint appeared for the third time as Tu Tze-chun stood under the West Gate of Loyang, gazing up vacantly at the light of the three-day-old moon as it ripped the mist to fine shreds.

"Were you speaking to me? I have nowhere to sleep tonight and I was wondering what I should do."

"So that's it. Poor fellow! Then I'll tell you a secret. Stand in this setting sun's light, so that your shadow falls on the ground. Dig where your stomach was, and you'll find a cartload of..."

Before the old man could finish the sentence, Tu tzu-chun raised a hand to stay him.

"I do not want any more gold."

"What, you want no more gold? Ah, then you have tired of luxury at last?"

The old man looked at Tu Tze-chun for some time, appraising him.

"It's not that I'm tired of luxury. I have had enough of people," blurted out Tu Tze-chun, unhappily.

"That interests me. Why have you had enough of people?"

"People are cruel and heartless. When you are rich, they flatter and adulate you, but see what happens when you're poor. Not even a tender look can they spare. When I think of that, I cannot see any use in becoming rich again."

The old man broke into a broad grin.

"So that's it. You sound no longer like a young man but like an admirably wise one. Well then, even if you are poor, you have found peace of mind?"

"No, not yet."

Tu Tze-chun hesitated a moment, then looked up resolutely and appealed to the old man.

"I want to become your disciple, and study the art of wizardry. Do not try to conceal the fact. You are undoubtedly a wizard of great virtue. If you were not a wizard you could not have made me the richest man in the world in one night. I beg you to teach me your wonderful art."

The old man remained silent for some time with knitted brows, thinking. Finally he smiled.

"Yes, indeed. I live on the mountain called Omei-shan, and I am the wizard of Tieh Kwan-tze. When I first saw your face, I could see that you were intelligent above the average, and that is why twice I allowed you to become rich. If you want to be a wizard so badly, I will make you my disciple."

Tu Tze-chun was overjoyed. Before the old man had finished speaking, he touched the ground with his forehead and bowed over and over again to Tien Kwan-tze.

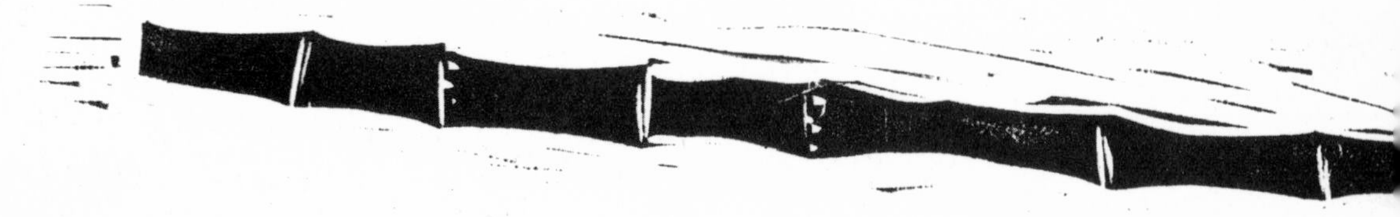

"No, do not thank me. Whether you become a good wizard or not is up to you. First of all, you must come with me to the far recesses of Mount Omei. Ah, what good fortune, here is a bamboo stick. We shall mount this and fly up to the sky in one swoop."

As the old man picked up one of the green stalks that was lying there, he uttered a magic spell, and he and Tu Tze-chun mounted the bamboo as if it had been a steed. And then, would you believe it, the bamboo stick bounded up into the heavens, like a dragon, and flew through the cloudless evening sky in the direction of Omei-shan. Terrified, Tu Tze-chun nervously looked down beneath him, but all he could see were green mountains far below in the evening light, and as for the West Gate of the city of Loyang, it was probably already hidden in the haze, for he could not see it anywhere. As they rode through the sky, Tieh Kwan-tze, his white sidelock waving in the wind, sang in a loud voice:

I stroll by cold north seas at dawn,
I walk in far Tsangwu by eve;
For boundless is the strength and brawn
Of the blue serpents in my sleeve.
Thrice I visit famed Loyang,
But not one man shall know I've been;
And as I fly o'er Lake Tungting,
I sing!

Presently the green bamboo carrying the two of them circled down upon Mount Omei. They landed on a wide, flat rock at the edge of a deep abyss. The place was exceedingly high, and hanging in mid-sky, there was the North Star, as big as a tea bowl. No man had ever set foot on this mountain; all was as silent as a grave, and the only thing that assailed the ear was the soughing of the night wind in the solitary crooked pine growing on the precipice behind.

Tieh Kwan-tze bade Tu Tze-chun sit down under the precipice.

"I am now going up to Heaven to pay my respects to the Goddess Queen Mother of the Western Heavens, and you must sit here and wait for me. Probably while I am gone, various devils will appear and try to decieve you, but no matter what happens, you are not to speak. If you so much as utter one word, you can never become a wizard. Do you understand? Though heaven and earth be rent asunder, you must remain silent."

"Have no fear. I shall not speak. Not even if I die."

"Very good. I shall be off, then."

Bidding Tu Tze-chun farewell, the old man once more mounted the bamboo stick and vanished straight up into the sky above the burnished peaks.

Tu Tze-chun now sat all alone on the rock, gazing silently at the stars. After he had been there about an hour, he began to feel chilly as the night air penetrated his thin clothing. Just then, an awful voice came out of the sky.

"Who is that sitting there?" it scolded.

But Tu Tze-chun did as the wizard told him and said nothing in reply. A little later, the voice boomed out again.

"If you do not reply, you will be killed," it threatened fiercely, but Tu Tze-chun kept silent, of course.

Then, having climbed up from somewhere, a tiger with fiery eyes suddenly jumped up onto the rock, and glaring at Tu Tze-chun, it let out a terrible roar. At the same time, the pine branch above his head rustled and shook violently, and from the top of the precipice behind came a white serpent as big around as a barrel, belching flames. But Tu Tze-chun sat quite still, not even moving an eyebrow.

The tiger and the serpent both eyed their prey; then, as if waiting for a chance to spring first, they glared at each other for some time, and in the end they both sprang simultaneously. Would he be crushed by the tiger's fangs, or singed by the serpent's tongue? Just as he thought his life was surely gone, both the tiger and the serpent melted away into the night wind like fog, and there was nothing there but the pine tree on the precipice, whose branches wailed in the wind as before. Breathing a sigh of relief, Tu Tze-chun wondered what would be the next thing to happen.

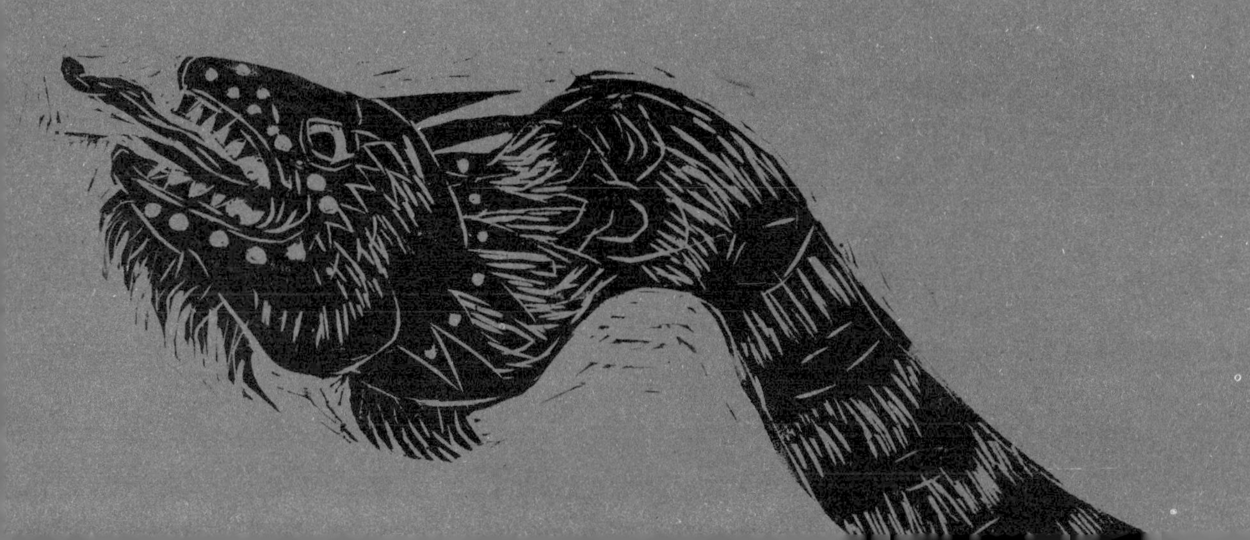

As he did so, there was a gust of wind, and a cloud, black as Indian ink, enveloped the rock, and a moment later, pale mauve lightning suddenly rent the darkness in two, and terrible peals of thunder began to sound. But that was not all. Rain came down suddenly, like a great waterfall. Tu Tze-chun sat calmly through this convulsion of nature. The sound of the wind, the torrents of rain, and then the incessant flashes of lightning—for a while it seemed as if Omeishan itself would overturn. And in the midst of it all, there was an earsplitting crash of thunder, as out of a whirling black maelstrom of a cloud, a bright red lightning fell on Tu Tze-chun. Without thinking, he put his hands over his ears and threw himself down on the rock. But when he opened his eyes, the sky was cloudless as before, and over the mountains that towered in the distance, there was the North Star twinkling away, as large as a tea bowl. The terrible storm, just like the tiger and the serpent, must have been the pranks of devils who were taking advantage of Tieh Kwan-tze's absence. Tu Tze-chun finally began to feel a bit of relief, and wiping the cold sweat from his forehead, he sat down once more on the rock.

But before his sigh of relief had time to fade away, an awful war-god, thirty feet tall, wearing golden armor, loomed up before him. The war-god held in his hand a trident, the point of which he suddenly thrust toward Tu Tze-chun angrily, with flashing eyes.

"Come now, who are you? This mountain of Omei-shan has been my home since the creation of heaven and earth aeons ago. To set foot here alone without fear, surely you can be no mere mortal. If you value your life, reply this instant."

But heeding the old wizard's words, Tu Tze-chun was silent and kept his mouth closed tightly.

"So you will not reply? Very well. If you refuse to reply, so be it. My henchmen will now cut you to shreds."

The war-god lifted his trident and beckoned in the direction of the far-off hills. As he did so, the darkness was suddenly rent asunder and the sky was filled with countless soldier-gods, like clouds, all flashing spears and swords and surging forward to attack. Seeing this, Tu Tze-chun almost cried out, but immediately remembered Tieh Kwan-tze's words and kept resolutely still. When the war-god saw that Tu Tze-chun was not intimidated, his anger knew no bounds.

"Obstinate creature. If he refuses to reply, we shall have to kill him, just as we said."

No sooner had he shouted these words than the war-god brandished his trident and with one thrust, stabbed Tu Tze-chun to death. His laughter resounded all over Omei-shan as he disappeared into thin air. And as for the host of soldier-gods, they, of course, had already faded away like a dream into the sound of the night wind.

The North Star shed its cold light once more on the flat rock. The wind, as before, continued to sough through the branches of the solitary pine on the precipice. But Tu Tze-chun had long since expired, and simply lay with his face turned up to the sky.

Tu Tze-chun's body lay face upwards on the rock, but Tu Tze-chun's soul quietly left his body and went down to the bottom of Hades. Between this world and Hades, there is a road called the Way of Darkness, where all the year round, the sky is dark and an icy wind whistles blusteringly. For a while, Tu Tze-chun was blown along by the wind like a leaf and floated through the sky,

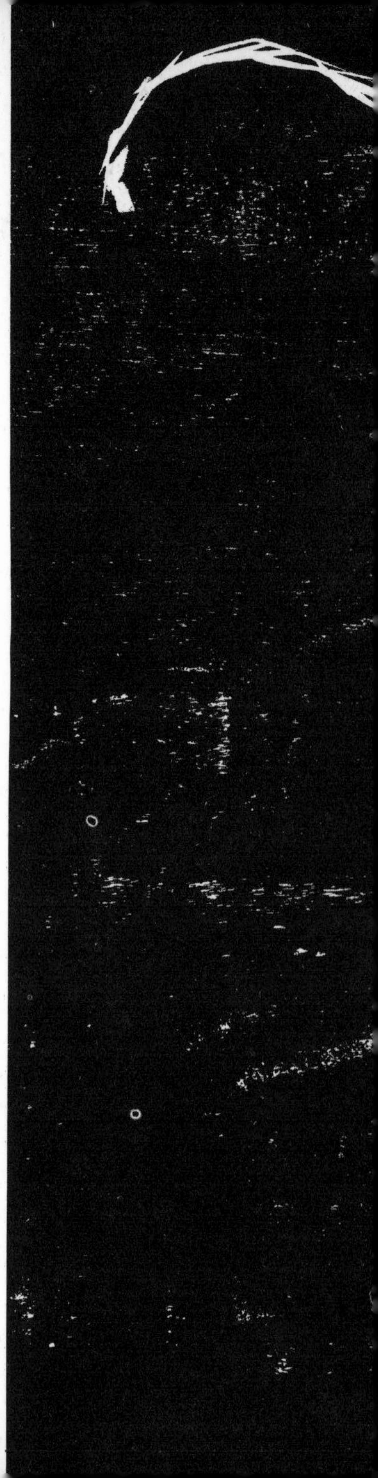

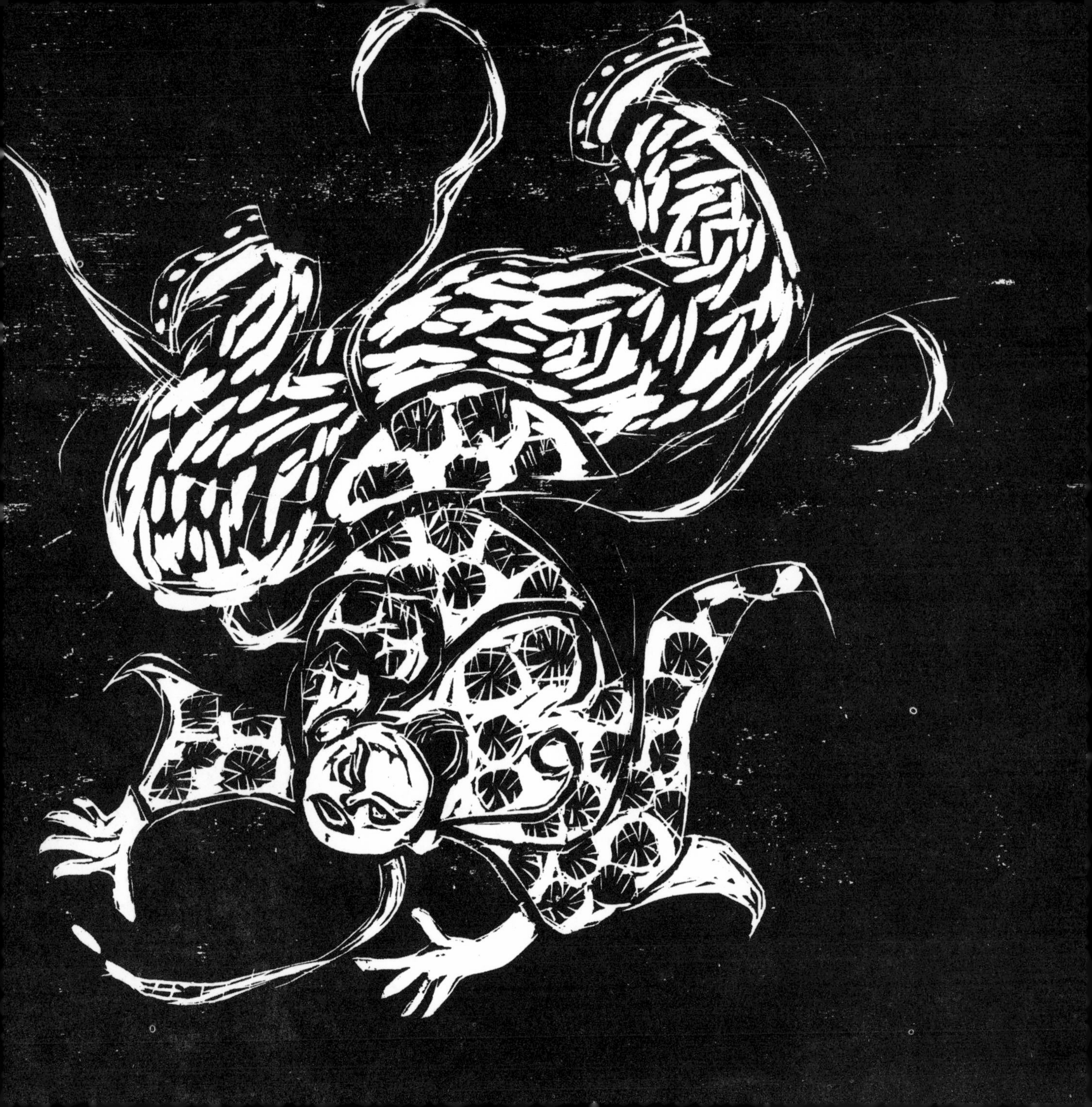

but presently he came to a fine palace hung with votive pictures. As soon as the demons who were gathered outside the palace saw Tu Tze-chun, they surrounded him and dragged him to the foot of a flight of stairs.

At the top of the stairs, a king dressed in black with a gold crown on his head sat glaring savagely about him. This must be Yenma, the great King of Hades of whom he had always heard. Wondering what was going to happen, Tu Tze-chun nervously knelt before him.

"What were you doing sitting on Omei-shan?"

Yenma's voice was like thunder. Tu Tze-chun was just about to reply, when he suddenly remembered Tieh Kwan-tze's admonition not to speak on any account. So he merely hung his head like a deaf-mute, and remained silent. Thereupon the King raised his iron sceptre, while the hairs on his face bristled.

"Where do you imagine this to be? It will be well with you if you reply instantly. Otherwise, without a moment's delay, you will be subjected to all the tortures of hell," he shouted ominously.

But Tu Tze-chun did not even move a lip. Seeing this, Yenma, the King of Hades, turned to his demons and said something roughly to them, whereupon the demons obeyed with alacrity, and prodding Tu Tze-chun before them, wheeled off into the sky above the palace.

In Hades, as everyone knows, besides the Mountain of Swords and the Lake of Blood, there is a valley of flames known as the White-hot Hell, as well as the Glacial Hell. Into these various hells, the demons alternately threw Tu Tze-chun. Thus he was mercilessly pierced in the chest with swords, his face burned by flames, his tongue pulled out, his skin peeled off, his body pounded with an iron pestle and boiled in oil, his brains sucked out by poisonous vipers, and his eyes eaten by crested eagles. If I enumerated all the miseries, it would be impossible to reach the end, so many and various were the tortures he endured. But in spite of it all, with tremendous self-control, Tu Tze-chun clenched his teeth and did not utter one word.

This naturally must have amazed the demons themselves. Once more flying through the sky, black as night, they came to the palace, and as before, cast Tu Tze-chun down at the foot of the stairs before Yenma, the King of Hades.

"This sinner refuses to speak," they reported in unison.

Yenma wrinkled his brow, and remained for some time deep in thought, but presently an idea seemed to occur to him.

"This man's mother and father have, I believe, fallen into the Realm of Beasts. Bring them here immediately," he said to one of the demons.

The demon mounted the wind and whirled up to the sky.

In the twinkling of an eye, he returned like a shooting star, driving two beasts before him. When he looked at the animals, Tu Tze-chun was dumbfounded. While the beasts appeared to be a pair of miserable, wretchedly thin horses, their faces were unmistakably those of his beloved dead parents.

"If you do not confess straight away as to why you were sitting on the top of Omei-shan, it will be painful for your mother and father."

But even this threat brought no reply from Tu Tze-chun.

"What an unfilial son! Even if his parents suffer, as long as he is all right he doesn't care!" screamed the King of Hades in such a terrible voice that the palace itself almost crumbled. "Demon! Take these two beasts and pulverize them."

The demons with one voice replied, "Yes, sir," and taking iron whips, they began to beat the two horses mercilessly from all sides. The lashes cut the air with lightning speed, and fell on the horses like rain, ripping their flesh. The horses—that is, Tu Tze-chun's parents who had become beasts—writhed in pitiful agony, with tears of blood in their eyes, and whinnying, so that one could hardly bear to watch them.

"Well now, will he not yet confess?"

Yenma restrained the demons from their beating, and once more invited Tu Tze-chun to reply. By this time, the flesh of the two horses was ripped to shreds and their bones pulverized, and they gasped for breath as they lay exhausted at the foot of the stairs. Tu Tze-chun was frantic, but remembering Tieh Kwan-tze's words, he kept his eyes tight shut. Just then a voice reached his ears. It was so faint that it could hardly be called a voice.

"Do not worry. Whatever may happen to us, if it is for your good, what can be better than that? No matter what the King of Hades may say, if you do not wish to reply, you must not."

That was most certainly none other than the voice of his dear, dear mother. Without thinking, Tu Tze-chun opened his eyes. He saw a horse lying helpless on the ground, with its eyes pathetically fixed on his face. To think that in spite of her agony, his mother could think of her son's welfare, with no bitterness toward the demons who had whipped her. Compared with his so-called friends who flattered him when he was rich and knew him not when he was poor, what a blessed motive! What fortitude! Forgetting the old man's admonition, Tu Tze-chun rushed headlong to her and put his arms around the neck of the half-dead mare, and with tears pouring down his cheeks, he let out a cry.

"Mother!"

No sooner did Tu Tze-chun realize that he had cried out than he found himself standing once more under the West Gate of Loyang in the light of the setting sun. The misty sky, the white crescent moon, the incessant waves of people and carriages—all were the same as before.

"Well? It seems that my disciple has failed to become a wizard," said the old man with the squint, suppressing a smile.

"Yes, I have failed. But somehow, I am rather glad."

Tu Tze-chun's eyes were still full of tears, and impulsively, he grasped the old man's hand.

"No matter how fine a wizard I might have become if I had not spoken, it was quite impossible for me to remain silent while those demons beat my parents with iron whips."

"If you had remained silent..." Tieh Kwan-tze suddenly became grave, and looked intently at Tu Tze-chun. "If you remained silent, my intention was to have killed you then and there. So now that you have no more desire to become a wizard, and are, no doubt, still weary at the thought of becoming rich again, what do you wish to be in the future?"

"Whatever I become, all I want is to live a decent and honest life."

In Tu Tze-chun's voice there was a light-heartedness that had not been there before.

"See that you never forget that, for we shall not meet again."

Tien Kwan-tze started to walk away, but suddenly stopped and turned toward Tu Tze-chun.

"Oh yes, what good fortune! I have just remembered: at the southern foot of Mount Tai, I have a house. You may have it, together with the farm. Go there to live as soon as you can." Then with obvious pleasure, he added, "Just now, all around the house, the peach trees are sure to be in bloom."